Udo Weigelt

Who Stole the Gold?

Illustrated by Julia Gukova

Translated by J. Alison James

North-South Books

NEW YORK · LONDON

Hamster brought his friend Hedgehog home to see his new treasure. But the hedgehog had barely opened the door when Hamster teetered, tottered, and toppled to the floor!

"What is it? What's wrong?" cried Hedgehog.

"My gold!" moaned Hamster. "I wanted to show you my pile of gold. But it's been stolen!"

"I see," said Hedgehog, who didn't.

Copyright © 2000 by Nord-Süd Verlag AG, Gossau Zürich, Switzerland
First published in Switzerland under the title *Wer hat dem Hamster das Gold gestohlen?*
English translation copyright © 2000 by North-South Books Inc.

First published in the United States, Great Britain, Canada,
Australia, and New Zealand in 2000 by North-South Books,
an imprint of Nord-Süd Verlag AG, Gossau Zürich, Switzerland.

Distributed in the United States by North-South Books Inc., New York.

Library of Congress Cataloging-in-Publication Data is available.
A CIP catalogue record for this book is available from The British Library.

ISBN 0-7358-1372-8 (TRADE BINDING)
1 3 5 7 9 TB 10 8 6 4 2
ISBN 0-7358-1373-6 (LIBRARY BINDING)
1 3 5 7 9 LB 10 8 6 4 2
Printed in Belgium

For more information about our books, and the authors and artists
who create them, visit our web site: www.northsouth.com

"You don't understand!" cried the hamster in despair. "It was right here in a glorious, sparkling pile. And now it has vanished! My precious treasure has been stolen!"

"Well then," declared Hedgehog, "we shall have to investigate."

So they set out to catch the thief.

The first animal they saw was Mouse.
"Did you steal something from my house?" Hamster asked.
"Who, me? I'd never take anything without asking," said
Mouse. "I wouldn't want someone taking something of mine
without permission. Let me come with you to catch the thief."

The next animal they asked was Ferret.

"Why is he hiding in that hollow log?" asked Hedgehog. "Hmmm. Very suspicious."

"Did you take something from my house?" asked Hamster.

"I don't steal!" cried the ferret quickly. Then he thought for a moment. "Well, actually," he said, "once I borrowed something without asking. But then I brought it right back because I felt just awful. Let me come with you to catch the thief."

They came to a tall tree. Raven sat high in the branches.

"Raven!" called Hedgehog. "Did you steal something from the hamster?"

"Me? Most certainly not!" cried the raven. "I couldn't care less about Hamster's gold."

"Well, thank you anyway," said the hedgehog. And they went on their way to catch the thief.

On the other side of the woods, they found Raccoon.

"Did you steal my gold?" Hamster asked him.

"Certainly not," Raccoon replied. "Where did you find your gold in the first place?"

"I got it out of the stream. It was sparkling under the water. I got quite wet in the process," Hamster said.

The raccoon thought. Suddenly he laughed. "That was no gold," he said. "It looks a lot like gold, bright and shining. But it's pyrite. Some call it fool's gold. It is not valuable at all."

Hamster was annoyed. "That doesn't make any difference," he cried. "It was my gold, and it was beautiful, and it was stolen from me."

The animals all thought about this and decided that Hamster was right. But they still had no idea who the thief was. They glared suspiciously at one another. Really, any of them could be the thief and just not admit it.

"Wait a minute!" cried Hedgehog suddenly. "I know who stole Hamster's gold. The thief gave himself away!"

The hedgehog ran off and the others followed as fast as they could go. Right through the woods they went, until they were back at the tree where the raven sat.

"You," said the hedgehog to the raven. "Are you quite sure you didn't steal something from Hamster?"

"Of course," cried Raven. "I already told you that I don't want Hamster's gold."

"And how do you know that it was gold that was stolen?" said Hedgehog triumphantly. "We never said anything about gold."

"Oh," said Raven carelessly, "I thought that since Hamster is a golden hamster, his treasure must be gold. But perhaps he just misplaced it, and the gold is not really gone? If I were you, I'd take a good look at Hamster's house."

"But it really *is* stolen!" Hamster protested.

The other animals decided to take a look—just in case.

Everyone ran to Hamster's house. Even from a long way off they could see something sparkling by the front door!

"It can't be!" cried Hamster, confused. "That gold was gone. Hedgehog saw it too—or actually, he didn't see it. This doesn't make any sense."

"Yes it does," said Hedgehog, laughing. "Raven tricked us. He knew that we were hot on his trail. So he decided to bring the gold back."

Just then Raven flapped down.

"You did take my gold!" cried Hamster. "Now admit it. Everybody already knows."

Raven looked from one animal to the other. The animals looked reproachfully back at him. At last, gazing at the ground, he confessed in a quiet voice: "I didn't even think about it," he said. "The gold was so lovely, the way it glittered. I just took it." He looked up at the animals anxiously. "How will you punish me for what I've done?"

Everyone looked at Hamster. Naturally, he should be the one to decide. Hamster thought hard. The gold had brought him nothing but worry and it wasn't even valuable. But still, it did look lovely.

Suddenly, Hamster leapt up. "I know what to do," he said. "Raven's punishment is to carry the gold to the clearing, where everyone can enjoy it."

"I'll do it!" cried Raven. He was so relieved that the heavy rocks felt as light as feathers.

That evening, they all gathered around the hamster's treasure. The gold glittered brightly in the last rays of sunlight.

"This is a glorious sight," said the ferret. The other animals agreed.

"All's well that ends well," declared Hedgehog. "Your gold may only be fool's gold, Hamster, but enjoying it together like this makes it a real treasure—far more valuable than all the real gold in the world."